This book belongs to

....

Quarto is the authority on a wide range of topics.

Quarto educates, entertains and enriches the lives of our readers—enthusiasts and lovers of hands-on living.

www.quartoknows.com

© 2019 Quarto Publishing plc

First published in 2019 by QEB Publishing,
an imprint of The Quarto Group.
6 Orchard Road, Suite 100
Lake Forest, CA 92630
T: +1 949 380 7510
F: +1 949 380 7575
www.QuartoKnows.com

A CIP record for this book is available from the Library of Congress.

ISBN 978-0-7112-4934-9

Based on the original story by Caroline Castle and Daniel Howarth
Author of adapted text: Katie Woolley
Series Editor: Joyce Bentley
Series Designer: Sarah Peden

Manufactured in Guangdong, China TT012020
9 8 7 6 5 4 3 2 1

MIX
Paper from responsible sources
FSC® C016973
FSC
www.fsc.org

Reading
Gems

Big
and
Fuzzy

QEB

On the snow was a house.

It was an igloo!

It was Sira and Ivik's igloo house.
They set off to fish.

Someone saw them.

Sira fished and fished.
Ivik went to sleep.

But someone big and fuzzy
was watching them.

Sira got a fish!

Ivik gave the fish away.

Sira got lots and lots of fish.

Ivik gave them away.

Sira and Ivik set off to go home.

But where were all the fish?

The wind howled
and howled.

Sira and Ivik walked
and walked.

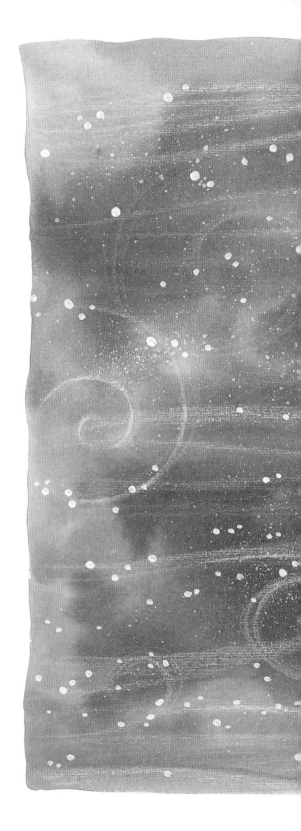

They got lost
in the snow.

Sira saw a cave. Sira and Ivik
went to sleep.

A fuzzy bear went into the cave.

The bear took Sira and Ivik back to the igloo house.

22

On the snow was a fish!

23

Story Words

bear

cave

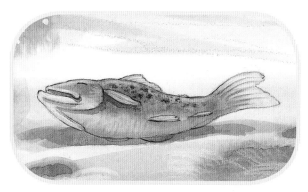

fish

igloo

Ivik

lost

Sira

sleep

snow

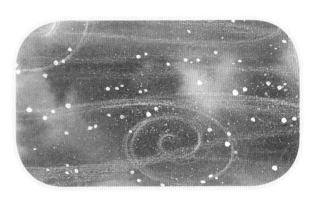

wind

Let's Talk About Big and Fuzzy

Look at the book cover.

Who is on the front of the book?

How can you tell that the story is set in a cold place?

What do you like to do when it's snowing?

In the story, Sira is fishing for food in the snow.

What kind of food do you like to eat?

What food don't you like?

In the story, someone is always watching Sira and Ivik.

Is this character mean or kind?

What clues do you see in the pictures to give you the answer?

What other animals live on the ice or snow of the Arctic?

How do the animals keep warm?

How do Ivik and Sira keep warm in the snow?

Did you like the story?

Who was your favorite character?

Fun and Games

Can you match the words to the pictures?

sleep   bear   walk   wind

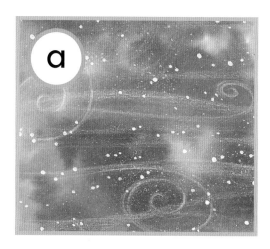
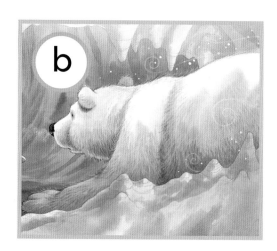

Answers: a–wind; b–bear; c–sleep; d–walk.

Look at the pictures. What are they? What letter sound does each word begin with? Follow the trails to see if you are right!

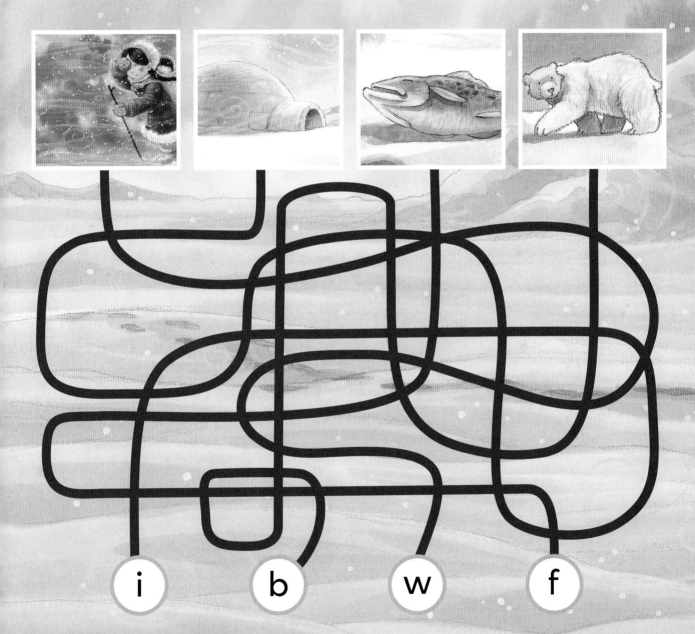

i   b   w   f

Answers: walk; igloo; fish; and bear.

Your Turn

Now that you have read the story,
try telling it in your own words.
Use the pictures below to help you.

READING TOGETHER

- When reading this book together, suggest that your child looks at the pictures to help them make sense of any words they are unsure about, and ask them to point to any letters they recognize.

- Try asking questions such as, "Can you break the word into parts?" and "Are there clues in the picture that help you?"

- During the story, ask your child questions such as, "Can you remember what has happened so far?" and "What do you think will happen next?"

- Look at the story words on pages 24–25 together. Encourage your child to find the pictures and the words on the story pages, too.

- There are lots of activities you can play at home with your child to help them with their reading. Write the alphabet onto 26 cards, and hide them around the house. Encourage your child to shout out the letter name when they find a card!

- In the car, play "I Spy" to help your child learn to recognize the first sound in a word.

- Organize a family read-aloud session once a week! Each family member chooses something to read out loud. It could be their favorite book, a magazine, a menu, or the back of a food package.

- Give your child lots of praise, and take great delight when your child successfully sounds out a new word.

Level 2

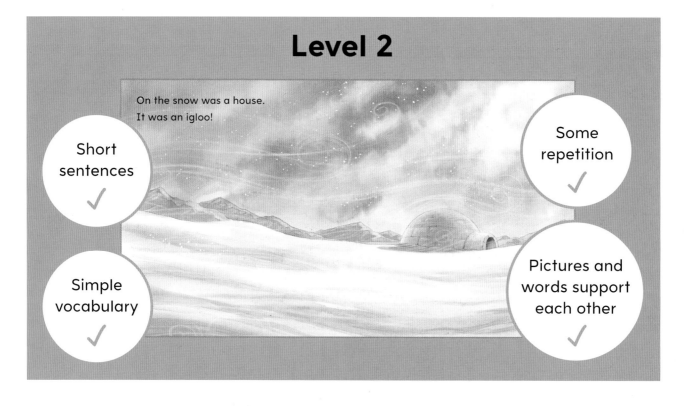

On the snow was a house.
It was an igloo!

Short sentences ✓

Simple vocabulary ✓

Some repetition ✓

Pictures and words support each other ✓